Mary's Cat

Kathleen E. Bardsley

Copyright © 2010 Kathleen E. Bardsley

All rights reserved.

ISBN-10: 1453804110
EAN-13: 9781453804117

Mary's Cat
Authors Note

---⋖❋⋗---

As a child, I loved stories about the Holy Family. I wondered how they lived and what they talked about. I wondered what life was like for Mary and what Jesus was like as a child. Even though scripture tells us little of Joseph, I knew he had to be special, too. I have studied all the Gospels and have done many scriptural, historical and cultural studies of life in the time of the Holy Family. This little book, Mary's Cat, is my attempt to tell a story of what life could have been like for this extraordinary family as seen through the eyes of their cat, Fearless.

I do want to be clear that this is largely a work of fiction. I have used the Scripture extensively for all references that exist regarding the Holy Family and Jesus' early years before he began his ministry. I have used and stayed true to all the references in the four gospels (for instance, Annunciation, the Visitation, the Birth of Jesus, the coming of the Magi, and the incident when Jesus' parents lost him for three days in Jerusalem) and I have to find a reasonable middle ground when they differed (for instance the location of the birth of Jesus, how long they stayed in Bethlehem, the escape into Egypt, and so on). This story is no substitute for the "real thing"—read the Gospels as often as you can, they will be new each time you read them.

I have also relied on Catholic traditions regarding that time and the Holy Family. For example, scripture does not tell us much about Joseph except that he was espoused to Mary and that he was a "righteous man" (meaning he was faithful to the Torah and respected). Catholic tradition tells us that he was much older than Mary. We do know that in Jewish tradition of that time, it would have been very unusual for an older man not to have been married. For that reason, and to be consistent with both the Gospels and the Acts references to James as Jesus' brother and multiple scriptural references to Jesus' "brothers and sisters," I have taken the creative license to make Joseph a widower, with a son, James. In addition, I have created an extended family for Joseph. The Jewish people placed great emphasis on family in those times, and it would have been expected for Joseph as head of his family to take in his widowed sister Naomi and her children. This big brood, led by Joseph, live together in this story as an extended family.

The references to customs of that time regarding marriage are accurate. Jewish couples were legally "married" but did not live together as man and wife until a year after the "espousing" ceremony. So, according to the Torah and in the eyes of the people of Nazareth, Mary and Joseph were married at the time of the Annunciation though they did not live together or have a consummated relationship.

We don't hear about Joseph after the "finding in the Temple." We do know that according to the scripture, at some point Mary joined Jesus in his ministry. She would not have done this if Joseph were still alive. So we can assume that sometime between the time Jesus was thirteen and thirty,

Joseph died. Catholic tradition teaches that he is the patron of a peaceful death. I have used those references to create the scene of his passing.

The boy Simon, whom they meet in Bethlehem, and the Roman lad Cornelius come from my imagination, but they will return in *Mary's Cat, Book 2*, "Pearl."

Lastly, my little cat, Fearless, is of course pure fiction. I don't know if Mary had a cat, but if she did, I hope he was as valiant and loyal as Fearless. He is a tribute to my sweet Flash, who was a gift from God to me, and to all the companion creatures God gives us to remind us of the grace and gift of pure love. I hope you enjoy getting to know him.

This book is dedicated to my three furry "lads" and all companion animals, to my mother Elizabeth De Witt Bardsley, who first taught me about Mary, my late dad Jim Bardsley, who modeled his life after Joseph, and my priests, Father John and Father Bill, and Rabbi Bob, who have all been great teachers to me. Lastly to my boss Sharon, and my groupies, Peggy, Gay, Pat, and

Mary Jane, you are my "strong towers"—
thank you and bless you all.

✣ ✣ ✣

Mary's Cat:
Book 1, Fearless

Chapter 1: The "Now"

It is a warm sunny day in Nazareth, and I am sitting on a ledge outside the carpentry shop taking as much sun as I can into these old bones. I am not the cat I once was. When I was young, my fur was thick and glossy and kept me warm even in the coldest nights. My vision was so sharp that I could see a mouse in the grass from far away. My hearing was acute, and I could hear that beautiful voice calling to me from across the village. My teeth were strong and could break a bird's neck in one sharp bite. When I was in my prime, I could run faster than the wind and jump higher than a bird could fly—well, perhaps not quite that high, but I was a great jumper. I can say with all humility that I was the best ratter in Israel and Egypt, if not the whole of the world. I could not be beat in a catfight. I was mighty in my time. But my time is almost done.

Mary's Cat

Now I am feeble; I can barely see or hear, and my teeth are almost all gone. She pretends not to notice, although now she feeds me food already mashed and carries me to bed each night. I sleep close by her side for the warmth and the companionship. Soon my days here will be done. I am content with that; I have had a wonderful and long life. Few cats have had such adventures as I. Now I cannot do much more than nap in the sun and dream of the old days when I was like my name: Fearless.

The Creator of all things has blessed me and soon will call me home. When I go, I will surely have made my mark on this small town, for it is populated with my progeny. I can see my eyes in one, my tail in another, and my colors in many. Some of the young ones still come to sit in the sun with me and hear my story. I tell them about the old days, how my life began. It is an unbelievable story even without embellishment, but still, my story is true.

I have had two names, the one I was called as a kitten and the one she gave me. Of the two, I like the second better

Chapter 1: The "now"

because it was something I became, something I earned, and something of which I have always tried to be worthy. I like to think of my life as beginning the day Mary took me from the tree and gave me that name. But in truth, my beginnings were much more humble.

✤ ✤ ✤

Chapter 2: In the Be

My mother, a beautiful, longhaired gray cat named Isa, gave birth to us while on a caravan from Rome to Palestine. I was born to a litter of eight kittens. I was last and least born: the runt. Not only was I the runt, but I was, by cat standards, quite ugly. My brothers and sisters would remind me that I was too ugly to feed as they pushed me away from my mother's belly.

I suppose it was true. My siblings were very beautiful: Sama and Maje were black with white stars on their chests, Doro and Benis were red and white, and Rufor was white and gray. The oldest and biggest of our litter, Janus, was a deep, rich gray like our mother.

I, on the other hand, was a mix of all those colors in strange striped splotches all over, as if I got the leftover colors. While each of them had beautiful slanted green eyes, mine were round and yellow. I looked

5

...manently surprised. While they had ...rfect, straight, white whiskers, mine were long, curled, and a mix of black and white. I even had a strange marking that looked like a mustache under my little black nose. To make it worse, under that nose was a set of "fangs" that poked beneath my lower muzzle. The whole, strange look was completed by my ears. They were almost bigger than my face, and my tail was longer than my body. All in all, in the litter of beautiful kittens, I was different, and my siblings never failed to remind me of all that I lacked in cat beauty.

My siblings tormented me constantly. When I tried to join in their play, they would gang up on me and crush me under their bodies. They would push me away from my mother so I could not feed, and later when we could eat real food, they would bite and scratch and hiss me away from the servings. When the mistress would put out the food, I would try to get there first. But never would I get more than a bite before they jumped on me and drove me away with their claws and teeth. I handled the physical pain they caused me, but much harder to handle were their constant insults. I was "uglier than a camel," "stupider than a dog," "useless and an embarrassment to the litter." The mistress named me Scrapper because I ate the scraps and leavings of their meals. My mother did little to help me and told me I would have to learn to live in a harsh world.

So I learned early to fend for myself. When the caravan would camp for the night, I would go out in search of food. If I do say so myself (and I do), I became quite an accomplished hunter. I would hunt mice and other small rodents and even a salamander or lizard if I were really hungry (reptiles tend to be somewhat chewy and dry). I was especially careful to avoid the snakes; snakes scared me. I saw one of the camel tenders bitten by a snake; it took him days to die and he suffered horribly. I decided that snakes were fast and deadly and very much to be avoided.

�֍ �֍ ✐

Chapter 3: Life Alone

As we moved from the desert into areas more abundant with trees and green things, I developed the fine art of "birding." I found birds to be challenging and quite delicious. Most birds in that area had not seen many cats before and so were not initially afraid of me. I would hide in the bushes in the early morning and wait for them to land on the ground to pick the worms. While they were thus occupied, I pounced. The feathers flew, but the birds did not. I had many a tasty meal.

One day I found myself far from where the caravan had camped. By the time I got back to the site, it was late morning and they had already left. I thought perhaps I should try to follow them, but then I wondered why. What would be the point? I would just be subject to more abuse.

I was now old enough to be on my own and had proved that I could take care of

Mary's Cat

myself far better than anyone else could, assuming anyone else was willing. So I found a nice territory to mark as my own and roamed it, gleefully wreaking havoc on the bird population. I later learned that my little kingdom was on the outskirts of a small hill town called Nazareth.

After a few months, the birds got wise to my tactics (birds have a very effective way of communicating, they never shut up!) and I had to be stealthier. I learned the fine art of tree climbing and could scale a tree in a matter of seconds. Birds put nests in trees and nests contain eggs—quite a delicacy, also known as "appetizers." While it was somewhat beneath my skill and cunning to dine at a nest, occasionally I did so when other prey was not available.

One morning I miscalculated how long I had been in a tree and was caught "in the act" by the returning flock. I retreated to higher limbs and got myself on one where I could not get off. The birds were diving down, pecking me, and driving me to the edge of the branch. I might have risked jumping down, but there was only hard, sharp rock below and I was quite high up. I was frustrated, out on a limb, and being attacked by my very prey. How humiliating!

I was howling like a baby when she first saw me, a very unfavorable first impression I am sure. I heard her before I saw her; her voice was like the bells on the harness of the master's stallion. Its timbre was so pleasing and light.

"What is going on up there?" she said. "How did you get yourself in this predicament, little one?" Then, low laughter. "Oh I see, the hunter has become the hunted."

While the observation was a little humiliating, it was true nonetheless and it was said without spite or meanness. In fact, somehow I knew from her voice that there was not an ounce of meanness in her. I hadn't had much use for people up until then, but that was the day it all changed. Somehow she shooed the killer birds away. I wasn't looking at her up until that point, as I had discovered that I had a massive fear of heights and was clutching a limb that was not going to hold me much longer.

Mary's Cat

She had a white head cloth that she unwound and laid loose around her neck. Then she swung one leg onto the lowest branch and climbed upwards until she was on the same level as me. She reached out her hand, "Come here, sweet one, and I will bring you down safely."

I could not move. I could only mew like a kitten. But she stretched out her hand. Before I knew what happened, she had picked me up by the scruff of my neck and pulled me to her chest. I was scared and started to struggle. She spoke softly and gently to me, wrapped the cloth around me, and tied the cloth around her neck. She began the climb down, all the time talking in that soft, sweet voice. I burrowed in deep and listened to the even beat of her heart; it calmed me, and I stopped struggling.

When she reached the ground, she sat on a rock and opened up the wrap. Her hands held me firmly but gently and she checked me for injuries, all the while soothing and stroking me. Her hands were magic. I had never been touched gently before by human hands. Though the people in the caravan had petted and fondled my siblings, they had no interest in me nor I in them. She said the most amazing things to me: "There, there pretty one" (me? pretty one?) "you are not hurt so badly, perhaps your pride has been pricked but your head is in good shape." She scratched my head and under my chin, and I was in paradise.

Then, wonder of wonders, she opened up the pack she had laid by the tree and fed me some cheese. I had never tasted such a thing before. It was amazing, much better than lizard and even as good as bird. As I gobbled it down, she gently picked the burrs from my tail and legs. "There, isn't that good?" she said. "And nobody had to die for you to enjoy it." Had I been able, I might have told her that the killing is half the fun of the meal, but I did not want to distress her.

I sat content and well fed on her lap, enjoying the easy stroking of her hand. She would not have been called pretty by my former mistress's standards, for she was simply dressed and unadorned. Of course

Mary's Cat

she was much younger, living in that tender space between being a girl and becoming a young woman. But I found her quite interesting. Her hair was long, dark and curly, simply tied back from her face with a piece of cloth. Her eyes, framed under dark arched brows were deep and brown, like rich soil. Yet they had soft golden lights in them that, in turn, lit up her whole face. Altogether, her face was like the flowers you sometimes see in the desert; they are so rare and beautiful that you are stunned by them and want to look at them for a long, long time. Humans bare their teeth when they are happy, unlike us cats who bare them in warning. When she smiled at me, it was clearly not a warning but more of a "warming." She was slim and sturdy as evidenced by her adroit climbing skills.

Most wonderful of all were her hands; they were so gentle as they glided through my fur. Her fingers were long and her palms and pads were somewhat rough, indicating she was not pampered. All in all for a human, she was more acceptable than others with whom I had come in contact.

As she scratched me under the chin, I did something I had never done before. A deep rumbling rose up through my chest and my whole body vibrated with it. It was rusty from disuse but it was purring for sure. It so startled me so that I jumped up and squirmed from her hands and ran a few feet away. She laughed and rose gracefully from the rock on which she had been sitting.

"Well, friend cat," she said, "I see you are done with me. I'm going up the hill to pick some herbs. If you wait for me here, I'll share more cheese with you when I am done."

❖ ❖ ❖

Chapter 4: A Most Strange Occurrence

I wasn't sure if I would wait or not, but the promise of more of that delicious stuff made me climb up on the rock she had vacated. My tail switched back and forth as I sat in the sun and watched her move up the hill. Her step was strong and graceful. Maybe I would wait, maybe I wouldn't. For now, my belly was full, the sun was warm on my back, and my face needed washing. I began my post-meal bath.

As I washed, I suddenly felt the air change around me, as if it were charged with a thousand tiny points of light. The scent of the air changed, too, incredibly fresh with a light scent of flowers and sweet candles. It was coming from where she had gone, so I leapt from the rock and followed her up the hill, keeping a respectful distance.

Mary's Cat

I could see her kneeling in a grove of trees looking upwards to what looked to me like a rip in the sky. Out of it poured a golden light that drenched her like rain. There was the faint sound of beautiful music coming from the opening. Then a creature began to form. It had great white wings, and at first it looked like the biggest and strangest bird I'd ever seen. Then it took shape and looked like a human filled with light and hovering over a rocky mount where Mary knelt. Its great wings gently swooshed the golden air around us, softly lifting the girl's hair from her shoulders. I knew this must be a holy place and this to be the most holy of moments.

You might think it strange for a cat to speak of "holy," but truly we were all crafted in the hand and heart of the same Creator. Cat, dog, camel, bird, fish, plant, humans, even snakes, we have all been made by the Master of All for his glory. Even the most simple of his creation (dogs) have no doubts as to his existence; we are born and serve in his almighty presence.

Chapter 4: A Most Strange Occurrence

I heard the winged one ask the girl if she would serve the Creator by bringing his son, the promised one, into the world. She asked how this could be done, as she was yet unmarried and had not been with a man. The creature smiled and said that all things were possible with God, and that God's Spirit would overshadow her and she would conceive a son. This child would be the Messiah her people longed to see. He then said something about her cousin Elizabeth and ended with, "For nothing is impossible with God." The girl bowed her head and replied, "Then let it be done to me as you have said."

The sound of bells filled the air. Then it was quiet for a moment, and the air began to stir. Golden light swirled around the girl, and for a moment she became the light. Gradually the light faded back towards the opening where it pulsed; the winged creature said a few more words to her and disappeared into the light. The tear in the fabric of the sky closed.

She still had a glow about her, and there was the scent of roses in the air, high and sweet, not cloying. I felt as if time had stopped for a moment, as if time itself had held its breath in awe. Then the world started to breathe again and the feeling faded.

❊ ❊ ❊

Chapter 5: I am Fearless

She knelt there for a very long time, head down, praying. Finally she rose and moved back down the hill, where I watched from behind a tree.

From the corner of my eye, I thought I saw stealthy movement in the grass of something gliding diagonally through the ground cover towards the path. It was a snake, a big, black and brown, slimy, shiny snake, silently but swiftly headed to where she would soon step. I mentioned that I stayed clear of snakes. They frightened me, and this was the biggest and most frightening snake I had ever seen. Its eyes were pure evil.

I started to quiver. I couldn't quite contain the half hiss, half "mew" that came from me. I knew it meant to bite her, bite her badly, and kill her, like the snake killed the camel tender in the caravan. I felt with all my heart that I could not let that happen,

Mary's Cat

even if it cost me my life. What was my life worth anyway compared to this special one?

   I leapt from my hiding place and moved faster than I ever had, faster than a cheetah, almost as if an unseen hand had heard my plea to protect her and sped me forward. As the snake coiled and pulled his head back to strike her, I jumped on him from behind, digging my four sets of claws and my long fangs into the back of his neck and head, snapping it backwards away from her ankle.

   The snake hissed with a noise like a thousand angry snakes, almost like a long howl, and thrashed trying to throw me off. I hung on, digging deeper with every claw and tooth I possessed.

   The girl jumped back. Just as the snake wrenched and dashed me into a rock, she grabbed a branch with a crook at the end, lifted the snake up into the air, and flung it. Though dazed, I am quite sure I saw the snake sail through the air as if hurled by a great hand and then explode into flame.

My head cracked on the rock as I fell, and everything turned dark around me.

In my last moment of consciousness, I thought that I felt the stir in the air of great wings, and deep, dark warmth cushioned me as if I were back in my mother's womb.

When I awoke, I was nestled in her arms. She was dabbing a wet cloth on my ear where a little blood dripped resulting from my fall to the rock. She was crooning to me and stroking me. "Oh you magnificent cat, you brave, beautiful cat, you amazing creature, what a service you have done for God and all mankind this day!"

I opened my eyes and blinked. Could she be talking about me? Magnificent? Brave? Amazing, beautiful? Me? I, the ugly, unwanted one of the caravan litter? I became completely limp with joy and with contentment. I melted into her. As I did, I felt all the longing and love I carried in me for so long me rise up in a great rumbling purr. I gave into the purr with my whole heart and being.

Mary's Cat

She smiled at me. "I can't call you 'cat' anymore. You must have a name of honor. If you will allow it, I shall call you 'Fearless,' for this day you were fearless in my defense. And if you will, I should like for you to come with me and live with me all the days of your life. I will need a fearless companion in the new road that I must travel."

I looked into her eyes and gave her a slow blink, the cat sign for "I will." She seemed to understand.

That is the story of how I got my name. But it is only the beginning of our journey together.

✤ ✤ ✤

Chapter 6: Our Journey to Judah

Mary carried me in the crook of her arm to her home. This was the first time that I had been in a town. This one was called Nazareth, and it seemed to be a busy place. I was glad to be in her arms as I noted a dog or two that I did not particularly want to meet. We entered a courtyard where a woman was wrapping loaves of bread and packing them into a cloth sack.

"Mary, where have you been for so long, I've been worried!" The woman rose as we entered. "There has been an emergency and you need to go to Cousin Elizabeth's right away. Elizabeth asked especially for you."

Mary's head cloth covered most of me so the woman did not notice me at first. Mary replied, "I'm sorry, Mother, but the most extraordinary thing happened and …"

Mary's Cat

As she started to talk, a man came out leading a small donkey. He spoke to her. "Mary, just in time. Amos is leaving with his family for Judah, we need you to go with them and take some things to your cousin Elizabeth. She has asked especially for you, says she needs you right away. Mary, the Lord be praised, it is a miracle! Elizabeth is to have a child!"

At that, Mary's mother, Ann hugged her. Before I could stop myself I let out a howl of indignation for fear of being crushed. Her mother said, "Why, what is this?"

Mary replied, "Oh, Mother, it is a cat, it saved my life, it was the most amazing thing ..."

Her father, Joachim cut in, "Mary, Amos is here. I am sorry but you must go now. I don't know when we will again have this opportunity for you to travel safely."

Her mother said, "I've packed your things and some food right here." Then the mother eyed me, "You can't leave that

Chapter 6: Our Journey To Judah

thing here, you will have to let it go when you get outside of town."

Mary held me tighter, "No, he stays with me."

Her father broke in again, "Ann, the girl must go now." He handed Mary the lead for the donkey.

The courtyard was filling up with a crowd of about fifteen people of assorted sizes and ages and more donkeys with packs on their backs like Mary's donkey. I hid under Mary's arm, burrowing into her armpit, and she held me tightly and determinedly.

He continued, "If they don't go now we will have to feed them all. Don't worry about the animal, it will likely run away when it gets the chance." There were more hurried hugs and then off we went in a cloud of dust.

Most everyone walked. From time to time, a grumpy, sleepy child would be lifted to the back of donkey, but for the most part a determined if leisurely pace

Mary's Cat

was set and most complied. After I got used to the noise, I poked my head out for a better look and then Mary let me crawl up on her shoulder. The people had begun making that noise they called "singing." I can't say I liked the sound too much, but the cadence and movement was quite lulling. I fell asleep wrapped around Mary's neck like a scarf.

A few days later we arrived in Judah. It was much larger and noisier than Nazareth and there were dogs about, so I crawled back onto Mary's arm where I could view this new place from under the safety of her cloak. One of the men walked Mary to her cousin Elizabeth's gate and left us there so he could return to the rest of the group that was now camping on the other side of town.

When we entered into the courtyard we heard singing. What the singer lacked in voice she made up for in joyous contentment. As we passed into the doorway, Mary called out, "Cousin Elizabeth? Where are you?"

"Mary!" It was the voice of the singer. I heard her steps first and then saw an aging woman, perhaps a little older than Mary's mother, come towards us. Mary swung me down from my perch on her arm and gently placed me on the windowsill. I must say that I was a little miffed at being put down, but then I noticed that the woman walked awkwardly and perhaps Mary meant to help her. As I looked at the woman I was astounded to realize that she was quite obviously breeding. Even though I am only a cat, I am somewhat acquainted with the general workings of human bodies. This woman, at least to my experience, was quite old to be reproducing.

When she saw Mary, her face glowed, her eyes sparkled, and she moved with a speed and grace of which I would not have thought her to be capable. Then, as she passed under a beam of light from the window above, she moved her hands to her massive belly and looked at Mary, wide eyed and open mouthed.

She threw her arms around Mary and held her close. (I was glad I had been let

Mary's Cat

down to my new perch, I would have been squashed like a bug!)

"Oh Mary, you are the most blessed girl and blessed is the child you are going to have I don't deserve to be a part of your joy but I am so glad that I am!" She took Mary's hand and held it to her swollen belly, "The moment I heard your voice, the child in my belly seemed to leap in me for joy." She pulled Mary back into her arms and then cupped her face and looked into her eyes. "You are especially blessed because you believed that what you were told by the Lord would occur just as he promised his people."

Mary's eyes opened wide then filled with tears. "Oh cousin, you don't know what good it does my heart to hear you say that. It makes my soul sing praises to the Lord, for He has looked with such kindness on me, just a girl. It humbles me to consider it all; I might be remembered by future generations for what is occurring now. Our Lord has such mercy and kindness for all of us. He lifts up the meekest of us and brings down those who use their power for evil."

Chapter 6: Our Journey To Judah

They linked arms and walked together. I heard their gentle voices murmur as they moved into the courtyard. I was content to sit on the windowsill and doze for a while.

We stayed in Judah for about three months. Once the people of the house got used to me, all was well and my days were easy; eat a little, hunt a little and eat a little more, sleep a little, sit with Mary and Elizabeth as they prepared for the birth of Elizabeth's child. Most nights I would go off in pursuit of mice or rats and come back before dawn by slipping quietly through the window into Mary's room and joining her in her bed. I would start at the foot of the bed, but later ended up curling close to her shoulder. The sound of her breathing comforted me. I would lightly sleep, warmed by her side, keeping her safe from harm.

Elizabeth's child was born with much screaming and wailing. I stayed away from that experience. The woman was old, and it was not an easy birth. But the boy was born whole, and the woman healed quickly. The birth process seems much harder for humans, and all they get is one

Mary's Cat

(which they have to take care of for a very long time). Cats must be more advanced because we can birth several at a time in a litter with much less effort. By three months, the kittens can pretty much take care of themselves; cats seem a much more efficient species than humans to me.

Soon after that we made plans to leave Judah to return to Nazareth. I knew that Mary was concerned about returning home, and Elizabeth had suggested she stay in Judah until she delivered her baby. But Mary was resolute. She said, "I have nothing to hide or be ashamed of. This is God's work in me, and he will provide for me. I must go home and see my parents and tell Joseph. This is good news for all our people, and I will not hide it."

I had learned from their earlier discussions that Joseph was Mary's espoused husband. This meant that Joseph and Mary were legally married, but according to tradition they would not live with each other as man and wife until the end of that year, when they were ready to live as one and begin their family.

Elizabeth said, "But what about Joseph? He is a righteous man, honored in the synagogue. You and I know God's hand is in this, but for Joseph, this will be hard to take; if he disavows you, it could go very badly for you. I know Joseph is a good and kind man; but the Law binds him." According to Elizabeth, if a woman were found to be pregnant before she lived with her husband, it was considered a very bad thing.

Mary stood firm. "This is God's work, and I must trust in him to manage all things to his purpose."

Elizabeth sighed, kissed Mary, and scratched my head absently. "Well then, I leave you with my love and prayers to God and in the comfort of this strange little beast." She lifted my head and looked me in the eyes. "You take care of this blessed girl!"

I blinked a firm "Yes!"

❈ ❈ ❈

Chapter 7: Home Again

We left Judah and returned to Nazareth. When we arrived at Mary's home, I stayed close to her, ready to defend her against any harm or insult. That night I did not hunt but slept with her, listening instead as she prayed to the Creator to show her what he wanted of her and to protect the child from all harm.

The next morning she was dressed in her usual clothes, without the heavy traveling robes. Slim as she was, the slight rounding of her belly was obvious. She walked to the kitchen area where her mother worked. As they talked, their voices were low but urgent. Her mother cried out, then wept then hugged her. Mary's voice was quiet but firm. "This is God's work and he will provide a way."

Her father came into the room and the conversation started over with the same ending. The family embraced and prayed.

Mary's Cat

Her father said, "Oh Lord, we are her parents, you gave her to us to raise up as a righteous woman, but she is still a girl in many ways, and this wondrous thing is beyond our understanding. Our daughter is precious to us and to you. We don't understand what you are about, but our trust is in you. I commend my daughter into your care and our house into your service. Dear Lord, show us your way."

Shortly after there was a knock at the door. Ann went to answer it. I heard the sound of a new voice, a man's voice; it was low and warm like a purr. I followed Mary out to the sunny courtyard. She sat on a bench in the sun, and I leapt unto her lap where I could protect and warm the child within her. Her hands ran through my fur gently.

"So my fearless protector stays with me," she said. "I need you here Fearless, to comfort and sustain me to give me your courage. I do not have the words to tell Joseph what I must."

Chapter 7: Home Again

I heard the man's voice as he entered the courtyard. I couldn't help stiffening up and making myself battle ready. "Mary," he said, "your mother told me I could find you here; I am so glad you are returned, I missed you very much!"

As he moved into the light I could see that he was older than her by about fifteen years. I knew from Mary's conversations with Elizabeth that Joseph had been widowed five years prior and had a son. I hoped that this experience with life had gentled him and would make him open to what she had to tell him.

He was a fully grown man, tall by most standards and rangy, moving with an easy lope across the courtyard to where we sat. His hair was thick and brown, streaked by the sun, and he had a full beard. His eyes were a light golden brown and twinkled in the sunlight with warmth and ease. I immediately liked him and thought to myself that this was a good mate for her and would not judge harshly the strange situation of her condition.

Mary's Cat

He knelt beside her and reached for her hands, kissing them. I kept my place on her lap. "What is this?" he asked. "What an unusual and handsome creature." This made me like him more and I let him stroke me; his hands were those of a craftsman, rough and strong. "I have seen cats in Jerusalem," he remarked, "but they are rare this far from the city."

"He is my new companion. I call him Fearless," said Mary. "He saved me from a snake."

"Then he is my friend, too, for he saved something precious to me," said Joseph. "I will make him something special in my workshop."

Mary smiled. "Joseph, pull a bench near to me, I need to talk to you." Her voice was soft as she told him of the encounter with the angel and what had occurred to her as a result. Joseph was silent through it all, but I could see from his eyes and the set of his mouth that he was not convinced of the truth of her story.

Chapter 7: Home Again

"Oh Mary, much as I love you, this is madness. Why would God choose you, a girl from a backwater village, to be the bearer of the Messiah? This is not how it is foretold, it makes no sense. Tell me what truly happened, Mary; did someone take you by force, a Roman? Let me help you."

Tears were streaming down her cheeks and falling on my fur. "I have told you the truth, as God is my judge, Joseph," she sighed. "If it is not true than there is no truth left in this world."

Joseph stood; he had lost the buoyant demeanor with which he had entered. "This is too much for me, Mary; I can't believe it. I can't bring you into my house, it is against our Laws. I love you and it hurts my heart to do this. I have my son to consider and my sister Ruth's children. They live with me, and I can't expose them to this." His voice cracked; tears were now coming from his eyes, too. "Oh Mary, if anyone learns of this they will stone you!" His hands clutched his temples as if he would force the thought away. "I will arrange for a quiet divorce. I will talk with your parents about sending

Mary's Cat

you back to your cousin. No one need know. I won't see you harmed."

Though her face remained calm, her hands were trembling in my fur.

Joseph's voice held great anguish, "I'm sorry Mary, I had such plans for our life together. After my wife died, I thought my life was over, too. Then I found you." His voice choked. "There will never be another woman for me, never again."

He walked slowly away; I heard him talking with her father in the house, heard the sound of her mother's sobbing. Mary whispered, "This is the work of the Lord, he will not abandon us." I felt the child move gently in her belly.

That night I followed Joseph's scent to his home. I'm not sure why; somehow I thought I could tell him it was all true. Deep inside me I knew with great certainty that I had been given a part to play in the Creator's plan and so had he. Somehow he needed to know this. I did not know how it would happen, but I knew it would.

Chapter 7: Home Again

It was quite late when I found him sleeping in his room by the carpenter's shop. I easily jumped the wall and from it to his window, high above his bed. He was sleeping fitfully, tossing about and muttering, "No, no, don't hurt her!"

Cats dream too, so I knew what he was seeing in his mind. Suddenly the room began to fill with a soft golden light. I heard the voice of the winged one again, this time softer, "Joseph, son of David, wake!"

Joseph opened his eyes blinking, at the great light. "What do you want of me?" he said, shading his eyes with his hand.

The angel said, "Do not be afraid to take Mary as your wife; she is pure and undefiled. For it is through the Holy Spirit of God that this child has been conceived in her. She will bear a son, and you are to name him Jesus because he will save his people from their sins."

Joseph whispered, "I will do it."

Mary's Cat

The angel said, "Sleep now and go to her in the morning and take her into your home as your lawful wife."

Joseph fell back into his bed in a deep sleep.

Then the angel turned to me. "All of God's creatures are valued in his eyes. Go home now and keep watch over the girl and her babe, for even little creatures can do great things."

I leapt from the ledge and hurried back to Mary, jumping through the window and landing softly on her bed. She rolled over in her sleep and pulled me close. I could tell that her cheeks were wet, she was weeping in her sleep. I wished that I could tell her that everything was going to be all right. All I could do was warm her with my closeness and gentle her with my purring. I praised the Creator for his goodness and vowed again to stay fearless in His service.

✤ ✤ ✤

Chapter 8: A New Home

Joseph came early that morning. Within minutes, there was much rejoicing and hugging. He got down on his knees before Mary and, holding her hand, asked for her forgiveness. She gave it readily and pulled him up. They embraced and then everyone was crying, but this time it was for joy. Then they all knelt and prayed.

Within a short time, the official "coming together" marriage ceremony where Mary and I moved into Joseph's house occurred. It was quite a party! Joseph's older sister Ruth and Mary's mother Ann threw themselves into planning the festivities.

Ruth was a round and merry woman. Her husband had died two years earlier, and she and her children now lived with Joseph and his eleven-year-old son, James. I learned that Jewish families were large and included cousins and other extended family members. Most lived communally,

Mary's Cat

sharing courtyards and cooking areas. If a woman were widowed, it was common for her family or the family of her late husband to take her and her children into the home so that they all lived together as one big family.

Ruth was not in the least concerned about a younger woman coming into the household and taking it over. It was clear to see that she loved Mary and that Mary loved and respected her. Ruth's children, Joseph, Simon, Judas, Miriam, and Hannah, ranged from ages ten to four and were excited about the prospect of the coming celebration. After a few hisses and scratches on my part, they learned to respect me, and soon we were all getting along well.

Everyone pitched in to cook and clean and prepare. I had to be careful of my tail and cautious of the brooms sweeping through everything when I went with Mary to help. When the day came, the whole town turned out. I chose a place high in a tree over the courtyard to enjoy the event from a distance, venturing down only a few times to taste a few of the delicious morsels Joseph slipped me under the table. The celebration lasted a few days but due to the circumstances, not as long as most. Finally it was over.

That night, after everyone had left, Joseph led Mary to a large sleeping room; I followed at a discreet distance. "Mary," he said, "It has been a happy day but a long one and you must be very tired." He cupped her face in his hands. She looked up at him as he said, "This was my parents room and now it is yours. I hope you will be comfortable here and happy." He smiled down at her as he continued, "I will be sleeping in the room next to the workshop if you need me." He kissed her lightly on the forehead. "Things will work themselves out in God's time, so let's be easy on ourselves and trust him to show us the way."

"Joseph," she whispered, "surely God made you for me, for I could not be happier with his choice. Thank you for your patience with me and with all of these changes, I am truly blessed."

Mary's Cat

He walked her into the room. It was spacious with a nice window for me to enter and leave. The bed was made with new linens and soft blankets, there were garlands of greenery and flowers strung about, and Mary's clothes and belongings were already put away. Joseph had even made a little nest of blankets for me on the bed. It would do quite nicely for us both, I thought.

She took his rough carpenter's hands and lifted them to her cheeks and then kissed them.

"Sleep well my wife," he murmured as he walked out the door. Before he closed it he looked at me and said, "Fearless, you keep an eye on her and keep her safe from all harm."

I blinked twice to say, "Of course I will." And so began our first night in our new home.

❖ ❖ ❖

Chapter 9: The Calm before the Storm

We had settled in nicely with our new family with a few minor adjustments. I did have to set James's dog straight about who was in charge. It seems the dumb mutt did not enjoy it when I jumped on his back. My claws were fully extended into his skin, and I rode him like a bull rider around the courtyard. For maximum effect, I hissed and snarled in his ear. He yowled like a puppy and tried to shake me off, but I held on, digging in deeper until I jumped gracefully off him unto the tree to daintily clean my paws. Since then he has made no moves towards my food, and we negotiated a truce that is mutually acceptable. I even let him sit near me by the fire on a cold night. Dogs in their place can be useful.

Mary glowed with health throughout her pregnancy and, though quite large about the belly, was still light on her feet and

Mary's Cat

active as always. The colder nights made us cuddle closer, and I could feel the baby moving in her. I purred to it to let it know it was cared for and safe. Mary said that the baby always seemed to be calmer when I was nestled close. Our life continued to be peaceful and simple one, until the day the Roman soldiers came to Nazareth with a command that would change all our lives forever.

❊ ❊ ❊

Chapter 10: The Road to Bethlehem

Within a few days, Joseph and Mary were packing to join a caravan to a town called Bethlehem. Apparently the Romans were conducting a census of all the Jews and wanted them to return to their ancestral birth cities for the count. This moving around people for no good reason seemed silly to me, but the Romans were not to be defied. Joseph had to represent the family line and go to Bethlehem, the city of David, the great king from which Joseph's family was descended.

They required Mary to go, too, which was frightening as she was so near to her time. But Mary was calm about it. She told Joseph, "I feel as if God is leading us to this place. Let's trust in his reasons and his will." Joseph arranged to join a group that was traveling in that direction. The donkey was packed up and off we went on another journey.

Mary's Cat

I say "we" because there was no way they were leaving me behind. Joseph suggested that it might be safer to leave me in Nazareth, but I jumped up on the donkey's back and made it clear that I was going with Mary wherever she went. He finally laughed and shook his head. "I give up. It seems your shadow will follow whether I want him to or not. Let's pack some extra food and water for him."

We traveled for days with this group and saw many people who appeared to be traveling for the same reason we were. It was a long way to Bethlehem, over rugged hills, deep valleys, and deserts. We even crossed the river Jordan. It was exhausting, but through it all, Joseph kept our spirits up by singing psalms and telling stories. Mary sang with him, her sweet voice mingling with his deep tones. They grew in love and companionship, and I was happy to be with them.

Finally we made it to Bethlehem. My first impression was that King David must have been very prolific to leave so many offspring. This town was seething with people!

Chapter 10: The Road To Bethlehem

It was so crowded that Joseph was afraid we would be crushed. He kept one hand on the donkey's bridle close to its head and the other around Mary to make sure she did not fall off the donkey. I kept myself concealed on her lap, under her cloak.

Joseph searched for his cousin's home, but when we got there we found that he had left for a different city and leased the house to another family. There was no room for us there. This was very bad. Mary was quite exhausted, she was pale and in pain. We needed to find shelter right away.

While Joseph was calm on the outside, I could see that he was worried. We went from place to place only to be told the same thing—"No room." It was now dark and cold. I could feel the child moving anxiously in Mary's belly, and I was afraid for her.

Finally towards the outskirts of town we found an inn. The innkeeper, Saul, tried at first to turn us away, but Joseph, in desperation, persisted. "Please!" he said, "My wife is great with our first child and soon to give birth. Please have mercy on us!"

Mary's Cat

The innkeeper's wife, Naomi, heard him and pushed her husband out of the way. She came outside and looked at Mary. Noticing Mary's pale face, she put her hand on her belly. "You stupid man!" Naomi said to Saul, "This girl is in labor right now!" She grabbed the bridle of the donkey. "Don't you worry, dear girl, we'll get you to someplace nice and warm and quiet so you can bring that child into the world. Saul," she said to the innkeeper, "I'm going to take her to the stable. With everything going on in the city tonight, I think it is the safest place for her. Bring some water and some wood for a fire and bring some blankets. We'll take good care of this girl and her baby!"

The woman took a torch and brought us around the back of the inn. We followed a trail up the hill. I could see a slight light at the base of the mountain. The light shown from the cave to which she led us.

The cave was the stable for the animals they had wanted to keep hidden from the Romans. She called to the stable boy and he came out. "Hurry Simon, help me!"

Chapter 10: The Road To Bethlehem

She turned to Mary, "This is Simon, as fine a stable boy as you will ever meet."

The boy limped towards us dragging one leg behind him. He looked to be about James's age though smaller and less vibrant with health than James. His left leg was shriveled and bent and of little use to him, yet with a wooden crutch he was able to move slowly but deliberately. His smile was open and friendly, and I could see that he was not sad for himself at all.

Simon reached up to take the packs from the donkey as Joseph lifted Mary down. I was still in her arms, and I could feel her tremble in pain and fatigue. Naomi hurried ahead and built up the fire in the stable. She made a big "nest" out of straw and laid some blankets over it. Then she and Joseph helped Mary to lie down on it.

I leapt to the ledge and surveyed our surroundings. All in all, it was not bad. The stone walls of the cave kept in the warmth of the fire the boy had lit, which now Naomi was stoking with more wood. Inside the cave were some stalls for a few cattle and some

Mary's Cat

sheep that were now curiously watching us as they munched the hay in their mangers. I thought I heard the soft cooing of doves overhead, too. Most of all, it was blessedly quiet after the cacophony of sound in the streets of the city.

Looking through the small opening we had entered, I could see the stars shining brightly in the late night sky. *Yes, I thought, this will do quite nicely.*

Saul came with more blankets and a large pot of water. He also brought bread and wine. Naomi tried to put Mary in a more comfortable position, but I could see that she was still in pain. Naomi spent a few moments whispering with Mary and then turned to Joseph. "Her time is very near."

Joseph was frightened; he had lost his first wife and a second child during childbirth. "Oh please help us, Naomi!"

She patted his hands, "I have delivered six of my own and half the children of Bethlehem. It is good that you came to my house. I will take care of your wife and child. I can see that she is strong and healthy, and she will deliver you a strong and healthy baby. Have no fear, but trust in the Lord." Then she smiled, "But if you feel faint, sit down. I won't have time to take care of you, too!"

She turned to the boy. "Simon, go to the back of the stable and get the new manger you built for the calves. It is just the right size. Bring it here and fill it with the cleanest straw, then cover it with clean blankets. We will need a proper bed for this new baby." She mussed the boy's hair gently and watched as he moved off to do his part. She looked at Joseph, shaking her head sadly. "He is such a good boy and good with his hands. The other children are cruel to him because of his leg and because he is sickly. His family disowned him at birth so I took him into our house. He likes to stay here and tend to the animals; he is very good with them, and he will do all he can for you." Then she turned back to Mary who was moaning softly. And so it began...

Chapter 11: Oh Holy Night!

The human birth process is another example of why cats are the superior species. We are able to conceive and deliver litters of kittens far more efficiently and quickly than humans. It takes people almost a year to grow their young in the womb, they labor in birth for hours, and only get one offspring for all the effort. Ours are beautiful when born; theirs are red, hairless, and wrinkled.

Having said that though, the birth of the Mary's child was quite wondrous. With just a little help from the innkeeper's wife and some effort on her part, Mary soon safely delivered a boy whom she called Jesus. He entered the world, not crying as most humans do, but gurgling and even smiling, as if he were glad to be here.

Naomi wrapped him in a clean linen cloth and laid him in Mary's arms, and he cooed as he looked up at her. He lifted his

Mary's Cat

tiny hand to his mother's face and stroked it as if he were comforting her.

His eyes were dark and huge. They glowed softly as he stared intently at her as if to say, "Thank you for carrying me so gently all this time; it is good to see you face to face!" In fact the whole room seemed to glow with a soft, warm golden light that enfolded us all.

I felt such contentment; I know the other animals felt it, too. Even the humans seemed be at peace; for a moment it felt as if the whole world sighed with happiness.

"This is a special child," whispered Naomi. "How blessed I am to be in this place tonight." She pulled the boy, Simon, into the light, "Remember this night, boy, you have been in the presence of the Lord tonight."

Joseph took the child from Mary and showed him to Simon, "This is Jesus, bar Joseph, of the house of David."

Chapter 11: Oh Holy Night

The boy smiled and held him for a moment. He looked up at Joseph, and said, "Sir, he is wonderful."

Joseph said, "Thanks to the work of your hands, Simon, he will have a warm and proper place to sleep tonight. We thank you."

Joseph placed the baby in the manger box that had been prepared for him. I had to admit that as humans go, he was perfect. His head was covered in dark, curly hair, and his skin was pink and soft. His limbs were sound, and he was kicking his legs and waving his arms with delight. Though he was only a few hours old, I could swear that his eyes met mine and that he knew me—and then he smiled. I knew I would care for him as long as there was breath in my body. I knew, too, that even though I was just a little cat and of no consequence in this human world, that I would give my life for him.

You would think that would be enough excitement for one night, but there was still more to come. In that space of time

Mary's Cat

between the dark of night and the light of dawn when the morning star shines, we heard the barking of dogs, the bleating of lambs, and the voices of men. Joseph grabbed his staff and moved to the entrance of the cave. The boy Simon stood beside him with his crutch held in front of him like a weapon. I jumped to position myself in front of the manger where the child slept.

I could see men coming to stand before the entrance. Joseph said softly, "Peace be with you. What do you want here?"

One of the men moved forward. "I hardly know how to say this, it will sound so crazy, but is there a child here, a newborn? We were sent to see him."

I heard Mary's voice behind me, "It's all right, Joseph, let them in." She knelt before the manger, picked up the child, and held him to her breast.

I've seen shepherds in the past, not a generally nice lot. The reason they are shepherds is because they have less

Chapter 11: Oh Holy Night

intelligence than the sheep they watch. And they smell. They also drink too much rot-gut wine and are loutish as a group.

But these men were so quiet as they entered, so reverent as they knelt before Mary and the child, so humble. The man who had spoken before said, "It is he, of whom the angel spoke."

Joseph was startled, he said, "Angel? What angel? What did the angel say?"

One of the other men whispered, "It was many angels, not just one—the whole sky filled with them and with their singing. I will hear it as long as I live!"

There was a boy with the shepherds; to look at him you would have thought him simple because he had the slack face and vacant eyes the simple-minded often have. But his words were eloquent and his face shown with a rare light. He spoke, "The first angel said, 'Do not be afraid, for behold, I proclaim to you the good news of great joy that will be for all the people. For today in the city of David, a savior has

Mary's Cat

been born for you who is the Messiah and the Lord. And this will be a sign for you, you will find him wrapped in swaddling clothes and lying in a manger ...'"

One of the other men added, "And then there were many angels, singing: 'Glory to God in the highest and peace to those upon whom his favor rests.'"

The first shepherd spoke again, "So we followed their light, and it led us this place."

"You are welcome here," said Joseph.

Simon brought them some bread and cheese, and they each spoke softly with Mary and Joseph as the child cooed and smiled at them. The shepherds quietly left a few hours later, promising to bring milk, curds, and hides later that day.

When they had gone, Mary looked at the child sleeping in her arms then to Joseph and smiled. "I do not know what it all means, Joseph. Truly our lives are in the hands of the Lord."

Joseph nodded, his large, rough carpenter's hand gently touching the soft cheek of Jesus. "Then we are in good hands, Mary, very good hands."

The child wrapped his hand around Joseph's finger and cooed.

✠ ✠ ✠

Chapter 12: Our Life in Bethlehem

We stayed in Bethlehem much longer than I expected. The Romans had delayed the census and then there was carpentry work to be done for the new synagogue. Joseph decided that since we were required to wait anyway, he might as well work and earn some money for our requirements and to send home.

Though he missed James and Ruth and her children, he wasn't concerned about their welfare, as his cousin Isaac had moved into the house (with his new wife Miriam) in our absence to run Joseph's shop. They would provide for the family until we returned. Isaac had been living in Magdala but was unable to find work there, so he returned home to Nazareth about the time we were to leave. God's timing is always perfect. I knew when we returned our home would be full to overflowing and hoped there were no new dogs to contend with.

Mary's Cat

Joseph was very skilled and his talents were much appreciated in the building of the new synagogue. Though Saul had invited us to move into their house, we had decided to stay in the stable, as it was cozy and quiet and away from the hustle of the city. Joseph turned the little stable into a fine home, making walls to separate us from the animals and crafting a table and benches and a proper cradle for Jesus, as well as a sleeping place for us all. He even made me a small swinging door to the outside. I could go in and out as I chose, hunt my fill, and return later at night to guard my family.

On cold nights, I would leap softly into Jesus' bed, curl up next to him, and purr contentedly. His small hand would touch my fur as he slept. My life was blissful. Around Jesus I felt I was as good a cat as I could ever be. I never hissed or scratched at the sheepdogs or other animals.

Every day I would hear Joseph whistling as he came up the hill to our little home, and I would run out to meet him. He would scoop me up onto his broad shoulder and

Chapter 12: Our Life In Bethlehem

feed me some tidbits of meat or fish. We would meet Mary and Jesus at the door Joseph had built to the stable.

It was almost a year since his birth, and Jesus had grown and flourished. He was now walking and almost talking. His limbs were long and sturdy for his age, his face bright and radiating with health and energy. His eyes were still large for a human and an interesting mix of all colors, dark at the rims, golden in the center with flecks of green and blue towards the middle. They seemed to change with the light. I loved to watch him discover new things, and he was playful yet respectful of me and my tail.

Simon adored the child; he helped Mary tend to Jesus in between tending to the animals at the other end of the stable. Mary tended to Simon, too, making him good meals, sewing him clothes, and teaching him the scriptures. Most of all she lavished him with love and appreciation and he flourished under her gentle guidance.

From time to time the shepherds would drop in to see the child and bring some small gifts of wood or carved toys. Mary would make them a meal and the boy shepherd would play his flute, much to Jesus' delight. There was something about Jesus that made people smile and want to hold him and be around him. All in all, our new life was quiet, simple, and quite good.

✣ ✣ ✣

Chapter 13: Strange Visitors

One night, more strangers arrived. These men were as far from being shepherds as a cat from a dog. Three of them were riding camels, and they had several servants who were leading donkeys laden with packs.

The camels were draped in costly fabrics and furs and wore bridles of gold and silver that jingled and jangled as they loped up to our door. Even the servants were expensively dressed in fine robes and turbans.

But it was the camel riders who were the most astonishing. Their robes were magnificently embroidered in gold symbols, and they wore sparkling jewels on their fingers and on chains on their chests. Their large turbans were made of silk and secured with huge gems.

Joseph stepped forward from the doorway, holding a lantern, "Peace be with

Mary's Cat

you my friends, what is it you seek? Are you lost? Do you need water or provisions?"

Mary stepped forward into the light, holding Jesus on her hip, "How can we help you?" she asked.

One of the men leapt down from his camel and astonished Mary by kneeling before her. The man said, "Dear lady, we have traveled for many months following that star." He pointed to the large gleaming star that had been overhead the night Jesus was born and had now returned as if to celebrate Jesus' first birthday.

Two other men joined him; each was equally and splendidly garbed. They knelt before Mary as well. Joseph looked bewildered by this spectacle.

Mary smiled and said, "You've come to see the baby. How kind. You must be tired. Would you like some wine for yourselves and some water for your animals?"

Before I knew it, the beasts were being watered by Simon, the servants were

Chapter 13: Strange Visitors

settled around a fire outside the stable, and the grand men gathered around the tiny table sitting on the benches and serving Mary and Joseph from their stores of exotic foods. They talked long into the night.

The men were Magi, or wise men, and also kings of their small countries to the East. They told Mary and Joseph that they had studied about predictions and mystical signs that were written about in old texts hundreds of years ago. These signs spoke about the positions of the stars. There were ancient writings that prophesied that a King of kings would be born and bring peace to the whole world.

One of the men was holding the sleeping Jesus tenderly on his lap. "This one," he said reverently, "is the one of whom the prophets and oracles spoke. His coming was written in the stars long ago."

I was sitting on Mary's lap, and her hand tightened in my fur. I remembered when we had taken Jesus to the Temple when he was still an infant. It was traditional that within eight days of the birth that he be presented in the Temple in Jerusalem if at all possible for a blessing. When we got to the temple, Joseph carefully counted out the coins to buy two doves, which would be sacrificed in the temple in thanksgiving for the birth of the firstborn son. People who were more wealthy would purchase a goat or lamb or even a steer for a sacrifice, but these small doves were all our family could afford. I wished that I had known. I could have caught some doves for them myself and saved them the money.

The Temple was very crowded. Mary held Jesus, and Joseph carried me in a sling under his arm. I knew that I had to stay quiet and hidden away. I observed everything through a fold in the fabric of the sling. As we were moving slowly through the crowd, a very old man in front of us turned and saw us. His old eyes lit up, and he pulled us to the side by a large column. He said his name was Simeon, and he asked to see the baby.

Mary let him hold Jesus. The man looked at him in wonder. He said, "Lord, now I can go in peace, you have kept your promise to me. I have seen the Savior you promised to your people. This child will be a light to all the nations and the glory of your people Israel."

Mary and Joseph were astounded. Simeon gently handed Jesus back to Mary, and he put his arm around her shoulders. Now his face was sad. He gave her his blessing and said, "This child will be rejected by many, but he will be the greatest joy to many others. The deepest thoughts of many hearts will be made known, and as for you, my dear girl, it will feel as if a sword has pierced your very soul."

Before Mary could respond, a very old woman joined them. She was Anna, who had lived at the Temple to pray and fast for many years. She heard what Simeon had said and began praising God. She told everyone that the promised one had come.

Joseph and Mary finally slipped away from the crowd to make their offering. We quickly returned back to Bethlehem amazed at all we had heard.

Now these strange men were saying amazing things about Jesus, too. The men stayed a few days. Before they departed, they told Joseph to be careful. They said that they had visited briefly with King Herod, who had asked where to find the newborn king. But in a dream, one of the kings had been told not to go back to Herod.

"Keep your eyes and ears open," he said to Joseph. "Be ready to leave on a moment's notice. I do not think the child is safe while Herod is alive."

Joseph took this warning seriously and had a pack ready to go if it were necessary. As it turned out that was very smart of him, for within a few months we were awakened in the dark of the night by an angel. The angel told Joseph to gather up Mary and Jesus and go quickly to Egypt. He said that Herod was in search of the child and terrible things were to occur.

✣ ✣ ✣

Chapter 14: Terror in the Night

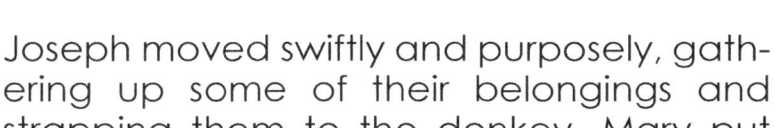

Joseph moved swiftly and purposely, gathering up some of their belongings and strapping them to the donkey. Mary put food and jugs of water in sacks and tied them to the straps.

Young Simon woke. "Joseph, what is it, where are you going?"

Joseph took him by the shoulders. "Simon, we must leave now. Very bad things will happen here soon, and we must get Mary and Jesus away from this place."

Simon's chin trembled. "Then let me help you so you can be on your way." He took his blanket. "Here take this, you might need an extra."

Mary turned to him and hugged him quickly, "No, Simon, you'll need it where we are going. We want you to come with us, if you wish, to be our son."

Mary's Cat

His eyes filled with tears. "But I will only slow you down."

Mary said, "You ride on the donkey and hold Jesus close under your cloak."

Joseph took the donkey's bridle. "Simon, your life may be very hard with us. It is your choice. I am sorry to ask you to decide so quickly, but we must go now."

The very air was bristling with something evil. I jumped on Mary's shoulder ready to protect her. Simon looked at Mary as Joseph lifted him on the donkey and Mary handed him her sleeping child. "I would die for him," Simon said.

"Let's live for him," Joseph whispered as he pulled the donkey out from the stable and onto the rocky path into the hills. "We will go through the mountains around Bethlehem towards the desert, away from Jerusalem."

The little donkey seemed to feel the badness in the air, too. It clambered with sure feet up the rocky incline.

Chapter 14: Terror In The Night

We had been moving up the mountain for about three hours when we stopped to rest. From our perch high up, we could see the city of Bethlehem like a small glow in the dark. Joseph said that we could keep going until dawn and then rest in one of the many caves that dotted these rugged hills. When we got to the other side, we would be in the desert and on the caravan route to Egypt; we could quietly join a passing caravan then.

Jesus had been very quiet. Now he was wide eyed, his gaze intent and sad as he looked at Bethlehem so far below us. In the darkness, I saw a deeper blackness hurtling towards that little town, something so awful I could smell its stench from where I sat.

I found myself shaking uncontrollably, my fur standing on end. Mary tried to soothe me, but I could feel the tension and coldness in her hands. She too was very much afraid. The darkness became a band of soldiers on horses; they burst into the town, swords flashing like hellfire. I could hear the screams, like no sound I had ever heard before. Mary had been holding Jesus, who now began to keen and cry. We learned later that Herod had ordered his soldiers to kill all the baby boys in Bethlehem under two years of age. Humans think that animals are vicious, but never has any animal in this world done such a terrible thing.

Joseph held Mary and Jesus to his chest, turning their heads away from the awful sounds below. I could see the tears in his eyes.

Simon whispered, "What is happening?"

"Evil is happening," Joseph replied, "evil of the worst sort. May the Lord have mercy on us for such evil. We must go. We must get Jesus far away from this place."

We hurried into the night in search of the dawn and safety, far, far from the city of David, now a city of death.

✤ ✤ ✤

Chapter 15: Into Egypt

While there were many remarkable things to say abut the Egypt and the city of Alexandria, the best is that they have a high regard for cats, which is to their credit. Also the mousing is quite good. There are many different species and all pretty tasty.

We were fortunate to join a caravan of craftsmen and their families who were going to Egypt to work on the great Library of Alexandria. We fit right in and passed into Egypt unnoticed. Joseph was highly regarded for his skill as a carpenter and a fine wood worker, and we settled into a Hebrew community in Alexandria.

We had a cheery little house. Mary was much loved by the neighboring women for her warmth and generosity. There were always children around the house, and Jesus had many friends. He too was well liked. He was a sweet child, who gave hugs freely and laughed often. He noticed everything and everyone, sometimes stopping his play to talk to an old man or give a woman a flower. When he was six, he began his studies at the synagogue with the other boys but far surpassed them in learning.

Simon had grown tall and strong under Mary's loving care, and he was learning the carpenter's craft with Joseph. He was well liked by the community and, at eighteen, was highly regarded as a "catch" by the girls and their mothers. Strangely, his leg had been healed during our trip to Egypt. One night, before we joined the caravan, little Jesus had started to fall. But he grabbed Simon's leg to right himself. Simon had winced but then picked Jesus up and hugged him. The next morning, Simon did not need to ride the donkey; he jumped up and walked as if he had always had two good legs. It was never much discussed, just accepted.

There were other such incidents of things righting themselves around Jesus. Sometimes I could swear the branches of trees bent towards him, offering the best fruits. Animals

Chapter 15: Into Egypt

were drawn to him, too. But it was not always a "charmed life" as some thought.

When he was only eight years old, a mad dog came running through the street, teeth bared, foaming at the mouth. I could jump into a tree, but the children in its path were not so agile. They stood frozen with fear. Young Jesus stepped in front of them and knelt to the ground with his arms open as if to embrace the beast.

I stood on my branch ready to jump on its back if needed to save Jesus. But the dog dropped to the dust, shaking and whining. Jesus laid his hands on it, stroking it gently, calming it. Some men had run into the street with sticks to strike it, but Joseph held them back.

Jesus continued to soothe the dog, which now lay with its head on Jesus' lap. "It's all right Father. He was scared, but he is all right now. He needs some food and water. He is very hungry and thirsty." Thus the mad dog became the good dog that would walk our blind neighbor to and from the synagogue each day.

Mary's Cat

You would think everyone would respond to such an act of kindness with awe or at least appreciation. But after Jesus healed the mad dog, some people looked at him strangely. Some parents would not let their children play with him, and he was seen as "different." I know well that to be different is not always a good thing. I would hear them taunt him or try to trip him. Jesus would face them down, but I knew it was hard for him.

Jesus asked Mary about this one morning as he was helping her prepare the day's bread. "Mother, some of the children are not allowed to play with me; some taunt me, why?" I could see that he was hurt, troubled by this.

Mary answered, "Jesus, you are different from most children your age. Some people will be threatened by that difference; others will be drawn to it. Above all you must stay true to who you are."

Jesus lower lip trembled, and I could see moisture in his eyes. He said softly, "But who am I, Mother?"

She hesitated. I think she knew it was not time to tell him all the circumstances of his birth. "You are my son, and you are your father's son. You are a good student but a bad baker. You have put too much salt into the flour."

She took a finger full of flour and touched his nose with it. He laughed and blew flour at her. Soon there was so much flour flying that I had to hide under the table before I became a white cat. I loved the sound of their laughter—and Mary's wisdom.

✤ ✤ ✤

Chapter 16: A Bad Cat

I have to confess here that while in Egypt I became a little too proud of my cat status. I had fathered many kittens and had gained a bit of a reputation amongst the other animals. I knew I was special and became very possessive of my status with Mary.

We had a large tree in front of our house where a pretty yellow bird came to nest. It had a sweet song. Mary thought it was charming, and soon it was flying about her head and landing on her shoulder. She would hand feed it little bits of bread. I began to hate that bird.

One morning after a long night of "catting" around, I was very tired and cranky and wanted to sleep on the window ledge. But the bird would not stop singing. It kept flying towards the window where Mary would usually greet it. Mary

Mary's Cat

had gone to help with the birth of a child, and she was not there at her usual time to greet the little bird.

So I greeted it. I jumped up and grabbed it in my mouth. By the time my four feet hit the ledge, I had broken its neck.

Suddenly a hand lifted me up by the scruff of my neck, "Fearless, what have you done!"

The bird dropped from my mouth to the floor. It was Jesus; he had witnessed my awful act. Jesus let me go and went to the little bird. He looked me straight in the eyes as he tenderly picked up the small, limp, yellow body and held it gently in his hands. "Fearless, I know that it is your nature to hunt, but you are not hungry here, you are well fed. You did this because of your jealously and anger."

Before he could say anymore, I fled from the house in shame. I knew I could never go back, could never face Mary or Joseph or Jesus again.

Chapter 16: A Bad Cat

I ran and ran and ran, but I could not run away from myself, from the awful thing I had done. I found myself at the docks and decided to find a ship to sneak aboard. I was sick at heart and hoped that someone would find me and toss me into the sea.

Finally I found a place in the docks to curl up and sleep, exhausted and brokenhearted. But somehow, when I awoke, I was back home in Jesus' bed curled up next to him, safe and warm. He must have found me in the night and brought me home. I started to pull away to run before anyone saw me, before I had to face Mary. But Jesus' gentle hand held me tight as he stroked my head with his other hand. "It's all right, Fearless, all is forgiven."

At that, I heard the sweetest song. I saw Mary standing in the doorway feeding the little yellow bird some bread crumbs. It was the very bird I killed the day before, trilling and fluttering around her.

She turned and smiled at me, "Come here, Fearless, I have fresh cream for you today." She held her arms open. I leapt into them purring as if my heart would soar out of my body.

I promised the great Creator that I would never again strike in anger or jealousy and that I would humble myself before all creatures. I have kept that vow to this day these many years later. I learned from this that a bad cat can become a good cat or at least in my case, a slightly better cat if he truly tries.

A year later, when Jesus was nine, Joseph woke up one morning and began packing up his scrolls. He said to Mary, "I had a dream last night. The angel of the Lord said that Herod is dead and we should return to Nazareth."

She smiled. "Home"—the word was honey on her lips. So we packed up our household.

Simon was now married to a Cyrenian girl named Sarah, and they had a little one. He decided to stay in Egypt and continue in the business that Joseph had taught him. After many tears and hugs, we were on our way home to Nazareth.

❖ ❖ ❖

Chapter 17: Home Again, Home Again

The journey to Nazareth was generally smooth except for one frightening event. We fell in with a group returning to Jerusalem. Jesus wanted us to go with them to see Jerusalem, but Mary and Joseph were eager to be home. We parted ways from the caravan and proceeded on our own path. Joseph promised that he would take Jesus to Jerusalem for the Passover the following year.

One night as my family slept under the stars, I grew hungry. Normally I stayed by Jesus' side at night, but I was so hungry I left him to find some little mice or lizards to eat. I knew I should not have left him, but the hunger would not let me go until I satisfied it. I found a big plump desert rodent and followed it, gradually drifting farther and farther from our camp. Suddenly I smelled something bad, something evil—a

Mary's Cat

snake! I could swear it was even bigger than the snake that had tried to hurt Mary.

I turned back and ran to where Jesus was. I could see the movement in the sand as the snake moved towards him. I let out a howl, a screech that would have woken the dead. Jesus jumped up just as the snake lunged for him. Joseph used his staff to fling the snake away, and it disappeared into a flash in the night sky. We huddled together. I was shaking, Mary was shaking, we knew what had just occurred and were terrified. Jesus seemed strangely calm. We decided to leave that place right away and packed up and fled into the night.

When we arrived in Nazareth, nothing had outwardly changed—but everything had changed. Joseph's son James was now a young man betrothed to a pretty, curly haired girl named Rachel. James had become quite the scholar and was now a scribe in the synagogue. Ruth's children had grown up, and Mary's parents had aged. Isaac's family had expanded and so had their business. They were eager to have Joseph back.

Chapter 17: Home Again, Home Again

We arrived at Mary's parent's door late at night. Mary's father opened the door cautiously then flung it open when he saw Mary. He held her in a bear hug, alternately crying and laughing as he called for his wife. Ann, her hair now gray and hanging down her back in a braid, threw her arms around them both saying, "Praise be to the Lord. Praise be to the Lord."

After a moment they realized that Joseph and Jesus were standing there. They hugged them and drew them in to the circle of warmth and light. I waited until the excitement was over and I thought my tail would be safe before I entered and found myself a warm place by the fire. They stayed up talking well into the night. Ann kept looking at Jesus, hugging him tightly, touching his cheek, and stroking his hair. His grandfather, Joachim watched him as if trying to figure him out. Jesus smiled but stayed quiet, answering questions when asked but generally observing things in that quiet way he had.

Ann told Mary and Joseph all the news of the town, the births, the deaths, the

Mary's Cat

scandals. She told how the Romans had beat down an uprising at Sephoris and how the roads had been lined with crucifixions. It sounded horrible. I thought, *These humans think that animals are vicious? We only strike out in fear or hunger but humans seem to enjoy doing the worst to each other.* I looked at Jesus, his tired eyes shining, his smile gentle as he poured wine for his grandfather. I feared for him in this angry, cruel world.

The next morning we returned to Joseph's house to start our life in Nazareth once again. At first, people looked at us a little strangely, especially Mary and Jesus. But after a while we fell into the routine of the village. Joseph was once again the master carpenter, and Jesus attended school at the synagogue like the other boys. But it was clear that he was not like them. He loved to learn and spent as much time as he could reading the scriptures and asking questions about them.

He would rather work with Joseph or help Mary than run through the streets with the other boys. It wasn't that he was serious

Chapter 17: Home Again, Home Again

or dour; on the contrary, he was kind to everyone and had a ready laugh.

He seemed interested in everybody and everything, but there was not a mean-spirited thought in his head. Never did a malicious word or gossip ever pass his lips. He liked to spend time alone, too. Sometimes I would go up into the hills with him. He would lie quietly in the grass looking up into the sky talking softly to the Creator, thanking, praising, singing, and sighing. It was a restless sigh as if something in him wanted to be released but was not yet ready. More and more his eyes seemed to see something I could not see, far, far away.

Yes, Jesus was a good boy and never caused his family any pain—until the time we went to Jerusalem as Joseph had promised him for the Passover.

Chapter 18: Lost!

Jesus had been beside himself with excitement about our trip to Jerusalem. He pestered everyone he knew to tell them about the city, the great Temple, and anything and everything else about the trip. The whole extended family, Joseph's brothers, Mary's cousins, aunts, and uncles, as well as many members of the town, would go together to celebrate the Passover in the Holy City.

I think I have mentioned before this custom that humans have of keeping their young for years rather than the more rational cat method of turning them loose within eight weeks of birth. Human males mature slowly and stay close to their mothers the first twelve years of their lives. They are considered a man sometime between twelve and thirteen years of age and then spend more time with the men, learning a craft and doing "manly" things. It was the Jewish custom that boys would become men at

Mary's Cat

age thirteen and take up the responsibilities and rights of a man. They would read the holy words of the Torah in front of the assembled community in the Synagogue..

In the caravans, women and men travel in separate groups, joining together for meals and for the evening rests. Because I travel with Mary, I travel with the women. More and more, Jesus traveled with the men on the way to Jerusalem and joined us at night time.

We stopped in Judah where Elizabeth and John joined us. Zachariah had died a few years earlier, and now Elizabeth was a widow. I could see that she had aged in the last twelve years but there was still a spring to her step and a ready smile on her face that mere age could not dim. John, at thirteen, was a tall, strapping lad, broad shouldered and lean. He had a long, fine boned, serious face and deep brown eyes that seemed to focus on something beyond this world. His hair was black, thick and long, and he already had the beginnings of dark facial hair.

Chapter 18: Lost

He and Jesus immediately became inseparable. John told Jesus that while the Temple was grand and beautiful, it was also corrupt in some places. He said Jesus should be aware that the Temple should be the house of the Lord, not of men.

Elizabeth confided to Mary that John would be leaving her to study and live with the Essenes later that year. The Essenes were a sect of the Hebrews that lived simply and severely, worshiping the Lord away from the distractions of the world.

Everyone used the time at Elizabeth's house to refresh themselves, clean up, and change for the short trip to Jerusalem. While we were in Jerusalem, Joseph kept me in a sack that he carried on his back. This was somewhat ignoble but necessary to my safety. The crowds of people were overwhelming. Hebrews from around the world came to Jerusalem for the Passover, and the city was bulging with bodies. The smells, the sounds, and the sights were all overpowering to me. I peeked out from my sack a few times but was generally glad to be safe and protected by Joseph.

Mary's Cat

The morning of the Passover sacrifice, we stood outside the Temple waiting to enter. It was especially crowded. Later we would retire to a friend's house for the Passover meal. Joseph had Mary in front of him and Jesus in front of her so he could see them at all times. A body pushed him forward into the crowd. Suddenly a stealthy hand reached into the pack in which I lay, likely thinking to steal from him. I bit it and scratched it soundly, and you could hear the thief screech even over the din of the crowd. Sometimes a bad cat is a good friend to have!

After the Passover was completed, we packed up to return home. It seemed as if everyone were leaving at the same time, and the streets were incredibly crowded. We finally made it out of Jerusalem and stopped at Judah to say farewell to Elizabeth. The next morning we were on the road back to Nazareth, tired and eager for the peace and quiet of our little home. I was exhausted and slept on the donkey traveling with Mary and the women.

Chapter 18: Lost

When it was time to stop and rest, Joseph came back to see us. Mary laid out the meal for the three of them. "Where is Jesus?" she inquired.

"I thought he was with you," said Joseph. "I thought he might be tired and had decided to take the slower pace with the women."

I could see that Mary was getting concerned. "No, I haven't seen him since the night before last when we were packing to leave. I thought he was with you. Didn't he sleep with the men last night?

"No," replied Joseph, "I thought he had gone off with John. He must still be in Judah! I'll go back and get him."

Mary began hurriedly packing up the food. "I saw John this morning and kissed him goodbye. Jesus was not with him. Oh Joseph, we've lost him! We must go back to Jerusalem!"

We immediately returned to Jerusalem. Mary was white faced with fear. Joseph

Mary's Cat

moved quickly through crowds, stopping street vendors or boys Jesus' age to ask if they had seen him. No one had seen the tall lad with the dark tousled hair and disarming smile.

By the third day we were exhausted. It felt as if we had been up and down every street in Jerusalem. Mary had barely slept or eaten at all. I was in my pack on Joseph's back when I heard that familiar voice. It was Jesus, and I knew it!

I scratched Joseph's back to stop him and poked my head out of the sack. I clawed my way from the sack to his shoulder and nipped his ear. "Stop!" I meowed, "He's here, I can hear him! He is near!"

We were in front of the great Temple. I nipped Joseph's ear again pulling his head towards the gates. Then I jumped down and flung myself through the crowd as I sped to the beloved voice.

Joseph and Mary ran after me. I leapt up the steps, and there sat Jesus speaking with some elders. They seemed delighted

Chapter 18: Lost

with him and he with them. I jumped on his lap, so happy to see him.

"Fearless?" he said. "What are you doing here?"

Joseph and Mary came up the steps. Mary's face was a mixture of relief and another expression, one I had never seen on her face before—anger!

"Jesus! Where have you been? Did it not occur to you that your father and I were worried??" Tears started to flow down her cheeks. She sagged against Joseph's arm, "We've been searching for you for three days!"

Jesus turned red, first from embarrassment, then blurted, "Why were you looking for me? Didn't you think that I would be in my Father's house?" Joseph winced. Jesus, feeling their hurt, was suddenly saddened. "Mother, I am so sorry, I lost track of time and everything else because I was so excited to be here. I have been learning so much, but that's no excuse for causing you this pain. Please forgive me." He put his arms out to both of them, and the three hugged.

One of the teachers who had been conversing with Jesus said, "It's our fault, dear woman. He has a rare understanding of the scriptures and great insight into what is truly important. We did not want to see him go. He could become a student here at the Temple if you wish it. He could become a great teacher some day."

Jesus shook his head. "No, thank you, my time here is finished. I am most grateful for your time and your teaching, but it is time to go home."

That night as we journeyed home, I sat up with Mary watching the stars with her while Joseph and Jesus slept. She stroked me absently. "I keep all these things in my heart, Fearless," she said. "I carry them with me."

✠ ✠ ✠

Chapter 19: The Young Roman

We made it back to Nazareth with no further incidents and life went back to normal. The next few years were quiet—eat, sleep, hunt, sleep, play, sleep, eat some more, that was my routine. That is, until one hot summer day.

It has been my life experience that when the Romans come to town it is generally bad news. The Romans are arrogant and brutal, and they looked down upon the simple folk like those of Nazareth. A few years later on that summer day, when I heard the thundering of hooves in the distance and felt their vibrations under my paws, I knew that nothing good could come of it. But I was wrong.

Mary and I were at the well filling the jugs with water to bring back for the evening meal. There were many women at the well, and they were talking as women do about births and meals and clothing. Most

Mary's Cat

of the men were in the hills finishing the planting or working in Sephoris. I was sitting on the ledge to the well, enjoying the sunshine, when I felt the vibrations and then heard the hooves. I hissed and arched my back as Mary pushed me behind her.

There were eight soldiers led by a man in a flowing red cloak who was clearly in charge. Following behind were a simply dressed, fair-haired woman of about Mary's age riding behind a soldier and then finally, bringing up the rear, a young man of about eighteen, who was barely able to hold onto his horse.

"Please, father, can we stop, please?" The young man was wheezing. He was covered in perspiration and looked ready to fall from his nervous, too big horse.

"Cornelius, by the gods, can't you stop whining?" The large man in the red cape turned back to look at the younger man. "You've been spoiled!" He glared at the woman riding behind the soldier. "By this one. You, boy, are soft as sponge, but this forsaken land will toughen you up, or kill

Chapter 19: The Young Roman

you." The man in the cape turned back to the soldiers, and they laughed.

The women of Nazareth had pulled back from the well but were surrounded by the soldiers. Mary calmly poured water from the well into cup and brought it to the man in the cape. "Sir," she said, her voice gentle, soothing. "Welcome to our humble village. It is very hot today, would you care for some cool water?" She handed the cup up to him.

He looked shocked then he laughed. "Well, 'humble woman,' you have courage!"

She smiled serenely and motioned for the women to bring water to the other riders. "Sir, you are our guests, and as such we honor you such as we can."

The man leaned down from his horse and looked sharply at Mary. "Woman, we are rarely considered guests. We take what we want."

Mary looked up at him. "There is no need here, sir. I can see that you are a man of honor who is used to giving orders and being obeyed. You have our respect, sir, and our hospitality freely offered with deference if you will honor it."

He swung down from his horse, "You are a wise woman. I don't find many of you in this miserable land. Well then, lead on."

Mary turned to one of the older women and asked her to take the younger girls to help gather some food and bring it to Joseph's courtyard. The courtyard was shaded by a large tree and often got a good breeze. There were tables and benches there that could be set up for food. I thought it likely that the younger women would be "replaced" by the older women so as to fade from the attention of the soldiers.

I noticed that the fair-haired woman who had been riding with the soldier had dismounted and was leading the young man's horse to the courtyard. She looked worried, and he looked as if he might fall off the big beast any moment. I kept a safe

Chapter 19: The Young Roman

distance behind the horses; big hooves can be unpredictable.

When the soldiers were wolfing down the food, Mary went to young man, who by then was lying on one of the benches away from the rest, wheezing heavily. The fair-haired woman was hovering anxiously over him. Mary touched the woman's arm gently. "My name is Mary. Would you like some bread and cheese?" She reached forward and brushed the damp hair off the young man's face. "He is feverish, I'll get you some wet cloths. Is he your son?'

"Oh no," the woman said. She spoke haltingly and with an accent I had not heard before. "No, I am just a slave, I was brought here from Gaul when I was but a child myself. His mother died when he was born. My child had died, and I became his wet nurse. He has always been ill. I take care of him. His name is Cornelius Junius. That is his father Maximus Junius, who owns me." She gestured nervously to the large man in the red cloak.

Mary's Cat

Mary touched her cheek softly. "What is your name, dear one?"

The woman looked startled to be spoken to so kindly. "My name is Vesta," she said softly. She did not look up, but I could see tears forming on her lashes.

"Rest, Vesta, eat. I will see to the boy." Mary dipped some cloth in the water and gently wiped the young man's face. He sighed softly. "I'll get him some lemon water, which will cool him and ease his distress."

Maximus strode over to where Mary tended his son. "Useless," he muttered, his lip curled. I wanted to take a chunk out of him. "My slaves are more valuable than this one; the gods must have taken my real son at birth and left this miserable piece of flesh behind."

I saw Cornelius's eyes flutter under his closed lids and a flush of red rise up his neck, but he did not say a word. It seemed that he was used to being treated this way.

Chapter 19: The Young Roman

Mary stood up and faced the Roman. "No, not useless, only tired and sick. He needs time to heal."

Maximas glowered. "No time for that, we are due in Jerusalem and must be quickly on our way."

Vesta leapt to her feet, "No master, he is too sick, it will kill him!"

Maximas turned on her, "You dare contradict your master!?" He pulled back his hand as if to hit her, but suddenly Mary was in front of her, her calm gaze meeting him directly in his eyes.

I was ready to jump and claw his eyes out even if it were to be my last act on this earth. But he put his hand down, looking almost shamed by the slender woman before him. Before he could continue, Mary spoke.

"Of course you must go, but why not leave the lad and his servant here? We can tend to him and when he is well, he can join a contingent from Sephoris. He can come to you in Jerusalem healthy and ready to be received as your son."

The Roman looked incredulous. "Leave a Roman citizen in this backwater town with you peasants?"

Mary's voice was calm, "Why not? As you said, he is of no use to you now. Perhaps it would be useful for him to learn about those whom he may someday govern."

Maximus shook his head, chuckling, "Suit yourself and keep him. I'll send for him in three or four months. Oh and if he dies, I will wipe out this entire town, starting with you."

Mary smiled softly. "He will not die, and he will return to you better for having been here."

Maximus shook his head, "You do have courage, woman, and I'll grant you that. If all Jews were like you, we would never be able to hold this wretched land." He swung around and called to his men. Within a few minutes they were off in a cloud of dust,

Chapter 19: The Young Roman

leaving behind a shaking Vesta and a moaning Cornelius.

"Madam," she said, "you don't know what you have done. He means it. I've seen them destroy entire villages!"

Mary put her hands on Vesta's shoulders and looked her in the eyes, "Fear not, Vesta, have courage. All is exactly as the one Lord would have it, and all is well."

By the time Joseph and Jesus returned from their work on the Temple in Sephoris, Mary had gotten Cornelius and Vesta settled into the house. Over dinner, Mary told them what had occurred. Joseph said, "Mary, I know your heart and that you cannot turn anyone away, but a Roman, and a centurion's son at that?"

Jesus listened to it all and then said, "We must take good care of him for his own sake, as well as for Nazareth. Perhaps we can learn more about each other. It's good that he is here."

Mary's Cat

Throughout the night Mary tended to Cornelius, giving him sips of lemon water and burning some herbs to help him sleep. I kept watch too, sitting with the woman Vesta as she absently stroked my fur. I could feel her begin to calm down and finally to doze.

Over the next week Cornelius slowly improved, still keeping to his bed. Each day he drank a little more and ate a little more, and his cough began to lessen. But he was sullen and withdrawn and would not speak.

One afternoon, Jesus was working in the wood shop at our home preparing some carvings for the Temple. He went into the room where Cornelius lay, staring listlessly out the window. "Would you like to sit in the sun for a bit?" Jesus inquired.

Cornelius turned slowly to him. "Are you talking to me?"

"I am. If you would like to sit in the sun, I'd be glad to help you. It is a beautiful day, better enjoyed in it than out of it."

Chapter 19: The Young Roman

"Leave me alone," Cornelius turned his head back to the window.

"I could do that, but haven't you been left alone long enough?" Jesus' voice was soft.

Cornelius turned back to him, "What do you mean? How dare you speak to me that way?"

Jesus moved into the room, "Why shouldn't I? You deserve to enjoy a beautiful day. Come out, there is a breeze singing in the courtyard and the leaves in the olive trees are dancing. It's a good day to be alive."

Jesus smiled and extended his hand. Without thinking Cornelius took it and rose from his bed. Jesus led him to a bench in the sun by the tree and brought him some water. While Jesus worked on the carving, the two young men spoke. I didn't hear what they said, but it was a different young Roman who returned to the house later. He seemed more at peace with himself.

Over the next several weeks Cornelius grew in strength and confidence. He was innately curious and spent the evenings after dinner asking Joseph questions about the Jews and their history. He would often walk with Jesus through Nazareth, meeting and learning from the elders. He stopped dressing like a Roman and wore the simple tunics of the workmen. He helped with cutting and loading wood, and soon became quite strong and tanned. He even attended Sabbath and learned about the Torah.

During this time, Vesta found herself with few duties. After a while, she met a widow in the town, Sarah, who suffered from aches in her bones. Her son had gone to Caesarea to find work, and no one knew when he would return. Soon Vesta was going to her home every day and taking care of her. Sarah became like a mother to Vesta, and she blossomed.

Mary watched all these things occur and kept them in her heart. She treated Vesta like a sister and Cornelius as a son. He was like a brother to Jesus, and the two of them

Chapter 19: The Young Roman

spent time late at night talking. For once Cornelius knew what it was like to be part of a family and to be loved. He thrived.

Such things must come to an end. Six months later, Roman soldiers came to Nazareth to "fetch" Cornelius. The young man they found was not the boy they had left behind. Cornelius was confident and strong, ready to take his place in the world.

He changed into his Roman clothing and first went to Vesta. "Vesta, you are free," he said, "in recognition of your great kindness and care for me all these years, you are slave no more."

She wept, "How can you do this? Your father will be so angry. I must come with you!"

"No," he said firmly, "I will tell my father this is my decision. Stay here if you like and have a good life, the life you so deserve."

Mary put her arm around Vesta's shoulder, "Yes, dear sister, stay with us."

Joseph hugged Cornelius fiercely, "You have become a son to me and I am very proud of you. Take care and don't forget all you have learned here."

Cornelius's eyes, filled, "I will never forget you, any of you; you saved my life and my spirit." He kissed Mary gently on the cheek. "There are no words to thank you," he choked.

Mary tousled his hair. "Stay well and remember who you are inside and know that you are loved. You always have a home here."

Jesus embraced him, "Don't be afraid of anything, for the Lord is with you, always. Go in peace, my brother."

Cornelius swung himself up easily on to his great horse, and waving one more time, rode off with the soldiers. I wondered if we would ever see him again.

❖ ❖ ❖

Chapter 20: A Great Sadness

Our life in Nazareth continued simply and sweetly. Jesus was now a young man, and I was a very old cat. My bones were beginning to ache some and instead of my nightly travels, I stayed in at nights by the fire or next to Mary, Joseph, or Jesus.

Under Joseph's careful training, Jesus had become a master craftsman, carving the most intricate designs into wood. Whenever a girl in the village was to be married, he would carve her a special wooden box to keep her most precious items.

He was well of marriageable age now himself, and it was clear the girls found him attractive. It was not that he was more handsome than any of the young men, it was just his demeanor. His smile was open and welcoming, without artifice. His hair was dark, thick, and curly like his mother's, and he had a short curly beard like most

Mary's Cat

of the men. His eyes seemed to shimmer with gold and green and brown. He saw beyond the appearance of people into their very hearts, and they felt as if what he found there was beautiful. He studied whenever he was free, and the rabbis had often told Joseph that they had taught them all they could and that he should study in Jerusalem in the Temple. But Jesus had no interest in doing that.

This is not to say that everyone in Nazareth liked Jesus. To the contrary, there were those who were jealous of his calm and easy demeanor. He treated everyone in a way that made them feel special. They thought him a dreamer, too unconcerned with the material needs of this world, too unwilling to join in their mean-spirited joking and pranks. I think they were afraid of him, afraid of what he saw in them.

He had stopped one of the shopkeepers from overweighing goods he was selling to a widow by gently pointing out to him that his finger was on the scales. The shopkeeper, angry at being found out, never forgot and spoke badly of Jesus behind his back.

Chapter 20: A Great Sadness

Jesus continued to treat him with kindness and respect. But I knew it bothered him that people went out of their way to insult him.

Though many of the girls liked him and would have been pleased to be his wife, he enjoyed their company but did not seek them out. Mary and Joseph did not press him. The rest of Joseph's family were all married and living nearby, so there was no lack of grandchildren. When fathers would come to Joseph to offer their daughters to Jesus in marriage, he would simply say, "It's up to Jesus, in his own time."

Jesus was now almost twenty, and most young men his age were long wed with children. I know bad things were said behind his back. I was still quick enough to claw an ankle and run away before being spotted, so I was able to respond to such insults on his behalf. I knew he never would.

It was late in the fall of that year that the worst day happened.

Jesus, James, Simon, and Judah hurried into the house carrying Joseph in a litter.

Mary's Cat

He was white as Mary's linens and blood was seeping from the back of his head. Jesus was calling to Mary, "Mother, Mother, come quickly, it is Father, he's been hurt!"

Mary came running out. "What happened, Jesus?"

They carried Joseph in and gently moved him from the litter to the bed. Mary grabbed her basket of healing goods and told Simon to get some of the hot water that had been boiling over the fire.

Jesus spoke. "Mother, it was terrible. Father was on the scaffolding showing Daniel something when the scaffolding started to collapse."

Judah added, "Joseph could have saved himself but he tried to hang on to Daniel. He swung him to safety as the scaffolding crashed around him."

Tears streamed down James's face. "Why won't he wake up, why won't he wake?"

Chapter 20: A Great Sadness

Mary's hands worked swiftly, feeling around the back of Joseph's head and neck as she washed away the grime and blood. There was a huge bruise forming on his chest and it was indented. Joseph was barely breathing.

I saw tears form in her eyes. "Oh, boys," she said, "this is very serious. You must get a physician from Sephoris, right away."

Simon said, "We asked the men to send one. We wanted to bring Joseph to you."

She touched her husband's face, tears still streaming down her cheeks. "You did the right thing; here is where he should be. James, call the family to come." She looked at Jesus and reached out her hand to him. "Son?"

Tears fell from his eyes, wetting his beard. He looked helplessly back at her. "Mother?" I knew from his tone, he could do nothing here.

Here was something more than a bird taken down before its time by a jealous

Mary's Cat

cat. Here was the passing of life according to a plan I could not understand.

I jumped onto the bed and crawled under Joseph's hand, feeling the warmth in it begin to slip away. I tried to purr to bring back the warmth. I thought of so many nights when Joseph and I sat in companionable silence in the courtyard after the day's work was done. As I sat next to him or sprawled on his lap, his rough carpenter's hands would become incredibly gentle as they stroked my fur and scratched my head and chin. He would talk to me about his day, and I would listen to his deep voice lulling me into a light slumber. We had been through so much together. I could not imagine life without this courageous, faithful friend. Truly, he was a righteous man among men.

The physician came, but, as Mary knew, there was nothing he could do. It would only be a matter of time before Joseph slipped from unconsciousness into death. The family gathered, wept and waited, and listened as each breath came slower, more labored. I kept my vigil by his side under his carpenter's hand.

Early in the morning, just before the sun rose, when the morning star was still the brightest light in the night sky, I felt his hand squeeze me gently.

"Mary," his voice was less than a whisper but she heard it and was by his side. "Beloved," he said as his eyes met hers, "every day has been a gift. I am a happy man."

Jesus leaned in, "Father?"

Joseph's eyes shown with love, and a soft white glow filled the room. Joseph smiled. "You are the child of my heart, my beloved son. Take care of your mother." Then he turned to James, "James, my dear firstborn, come and receive my blessing." He blessed James and then blessed them all. Then his hand rested on my head. "Fearless, my friend, how could I have made it without you? You take care of them both."

Mary's Cat

I felt a vibration in the room, and the sweeping of wings creating a soft breeze; I heard a sound like music, then saw a golden light. Joseph's hand fell from me as his spirit joined the light and became one with it. A great peace filled the room, and all were quiet. It was finished.

People from miles around came to honor Joseph's life. For many nights people would sit in the courtyard on the benches Joseph had hewn and talk about how he had touched their lives. Poor, rich, young, old, Jew, Roman, Greek, free, or slave, so many people came to speak of how his great kindness had changed something in them at the very moment when they were ready to give up. Many of these good works were not known to us. He had just gone about his life quietly doing good. We missed him deeply. There was a hole in our hearts that could never again be filled in this life. We looked forward with hope to the next.

❖ ❖ ❖

Chapter 21: And Now It Ends

So now my story comes to an end. I sit in the sun, listening to Jesus work in the shop. He has changed since Joseph died. He still works with James and the other men, but he often goes off by himself to be alone and pray. His eyes seem to be focused on something I cannot see. Though he and Mary have always been close, he is now especially kind and attentive to her. He brings her flowers or carves her special bowls and often walks with her to the well to bring back water in the morning. I feel as if he is giving her all of himself now to prepare her for something later.

Sometimes at night he picks me up and takes me out to the bench under the tree and we sit companionably under the stars contemplating the greatness of it all. His hand warms me from the chill that now invades my bones. When it is time to go in, he gently picks me up, cradles me in his arms, and carries me into Mary's room.

Mary's Cat

He leaves me on her bed, wrapped in his cloak. Someday he will leave Nazareth and begin his mission, whatever that might be. But for now, he is here and that is enough. In his presence I feel as if I am a very good cat.

Today is a beautiful day in Nazareth. I am sitting on the sun-warmed bench. Though my eyes have dimmed and I cannot see the birds, I hear them making a racket in the tree. I can hear Mary singing in the kitchen. She still sounds like the young girl who saved me a little over twenty years ago. I can hear the hammers from the carpentry shop. I can hear my heart slowing, slowing down and my breathing becoming shallow. Despite the warm summer sun, I feel cold to my very bones.

I am not sad. I go joyfully to face my beloved Creator. I am grateful for the gift of my life. To be Mary's cat has been my delight. Surely no creature has been as blessed as I.

I feel a warm breeze ruffle my fur. I hear the sound of singing. Through my closed

Chapter 21: And Now It Ends

eyelids I see a blazing golden light. I feel a rough carpenter's hand caress my face. Then the voice from the light that I heard so long ago says, "Welcome home, good and faithful servant." With the last of my strength, I purr. I surrender myself to the light.

I am not afraid. I am Fearless.

✣ ✣ ✣

Made in United States
Orlando, FL
03 April 2022